I turned and ran into a space in the box, taking two defenders with me. Lily looked up and curled in a cross. It sailed past me and the defenders and landed at Chris's feet. Chris controlled it well but didn't shoot. Instead he saw Gurinder running out of his goal to reach him. Chris twisted left and then right and then passed the ball into a space.

I turned my marker and stuck my foot out. The ball flicked up and looked like it was heading into the goal. I spun round to celebrate, but I was too early. The ball had hit the post!

Read every book in this action-packed

football series!

STARTING ELEVEN

MISSING!

STARS!

GLORY!

SOCCER SQUAD

SQUAD

GLORY!

Bali Rai

Illustrated by Mike Phillips

RED FOX

SOCCER SQUAD: GLORY!
A RED FOX BOOK 978 1 862 30656 1

Published in Great Britain by Red Fox,
an imprint of Random House Children's Books
A Random House Group Company

This edition published 2009

1 3 5 7 9 10 8 6 4 2

The Random House Group Limited supports the Forest Stewardship Council (FSC), the
leading international forest certification organization. All our titles that are printed on
Greenpeace-approved FSC-certified paper carry the FSC logo. Our paper procurement
policy can be found at www.rbooks.co.uk/environment.

Set in 14/22pt Meta Normal

Red Fox Books are published by Random House Children's Books,
61–63 Uxbridge Road, London W5 5SA

www.**kids**at**randomhouse**.co.uk
www.**rbooks**.co.uk

Addresses for companies within The Random House Group Limited can be found at:
www.randomhouse.co.uk/offices.htm

THE RANDOM HOUSE GROUP Limited Reg. No. 954009

A CIP catalogue record for this book is available from the British Library.

Printed in the UK by CPI Bookmarque, Croydon, CR0 4TD

GLORY!

Chapter 1

Thursday

'Cabbage-faced glory hunter!'

Dal, who is one of my best mates, shook his head at me. I grinned and took the ball from him.

'Come on, Abs,' he replied. 'You can come up with better than that!'

We both play for a team called Rushton Reds and Thursday nights are training nights. Dal goes to the same school as me, along with two other lads, Jason and Chris. They play for the Reds too and they were standing next to us as we practised keep-ups. Dal is about my height with short brown hair and he's really stocky. He thinks he's the best at keep-ups too!

'How many did you just manage?' I asked him.

'Twenty,' he told me.

I picked up the ball and then let it drop towards my right foot. As it dropped I stopped it from hitting the ground by juggling it with my foot. I counted up to ten and then Chris shouted something and I lost concentration.

'CHRIS!' I yelled.

'See?' said Dal, laughing at me. 'Rubbish!'

As I tried again some of the other players came over to us. The thing is . . . well, Rushton Reds aren't like a normal football team. Instead of just boys playing, we have girls too. When they first started playing with us, I didn't like it. But now I think they're great. We call them the Barbies for a laugh. And they call *us* the Smellies . . . Now two of them, Lily and Parvy, stood and watched my second attempt to beat Dal's keep-up score. I'd managed fifteen when Lily started to giggle. I lost concentration again and the ball hit my shin and flew off.

'LILY!'

'I'm sorry,' she told me. 'It's just that you pull really funny faces when you concentrate . . .'

I looked at Dal to see if he thought I looked funny too. He smiled at me.

'You do look a bit funny,' he said.

'No, I don't,' I replied.

'Yes, you do . . .' added Parvy.

For a split second I got a bit annoyed, but then I just smiled.

'Go and play with your hair, Barbie,' I said.

'OK, REDS!' shouted one of our three coaches, Ian. 'Time for a practice game . . .'

I went and got the ball and returned to stand with my friends. Our chief coach is called Steve and he's just come out of hospital so we were working today with Ian and our third coach, Wendy, who used to run the girls team only. She's American. She came over and sorted the squad out into two teams.

'We're doing things a little differently, y'all,' she told us. 'Because we have a Cup game on Saturday, we're going to work on defensive and attacking drills today . . .'

'Yay!' shouted Lily, who likes nothing better than playing up front. And I've got to admit it, she's really good too.

'I bet I can score more goals than you!' I told her.

'In your dreams, Smelly!' she replied.

Wendy handed out the vests – red for the attackers and blue for the defenders. I got a red one because I play as a striker, and Lily and Chris got red ones too. Dal, Parvy and Jason were on the blue team, with the rest of the squad split evenly. We had a new girl with us too, Olivia. She was the twin sister of one of the lads in the team. He's called Corky. Olivia was playing in attack with my team.

'Have you played much before?' I asked her as Wendy gave the defenders instructions.

Olivia nodded. 'I used to play for a team, too, but they broke up,' she told me.

'As a striker?' I added.

'Yeah – I love scoring goals!' she said.

I nodded in agreement. I loved scoring goals too. Lots and lots of goals!

'Lily's good,' I told her. 'And Chris.'

'I like Lily's boots,' replied Olivia. 'They're really bright!'

She was right. Lily's boots were orange with green stripes on them. Lily noticed that we were looking at them and she came straight over.

'They're nice, aren't they?' she said to us.

Me and Olivia nodded.

'I call them my glory boots,' Lily went on. 'They're going to bring me lots of luck!'

I gave her a funny look. 'How do you know that?' I asked.

'Because I'm a soccer *ninja*,' she replied before winking at Olivia.

I'd heard the girls talking about soccer ninjas before, but I had no idea what they meant. I asked Lily.

'Oh, it's nothing for you to worry about,' she said to me, sounding a lot like my mum when she doesn't want me to ask questions about stuff.

'Tell me!' I pleaded.

Lily shook her head. 'Can't,' she told me. 'It's rule ten of the soccer ninja code. Anyone who tells the Secrets of the Way to

the wrong person loses the skills . . .'

Olivia started giggling.

'Do you know what it means?' I asked her.

'*Yeah!*' she replied. 'It's a girl thing . . .'

'Oh, keep it then!' I told them, pretending to get upset. But I wasn't really upset at all. They were just messing about.

Wendy blew on her whistle and we took up our positions.

After the practice, me, Chris, Jason and Dal walked home together. We live in the same area and it was a really warm evening so we didn't mind walking. Jason was talking about how well Chelsea FC were doing in the Premier League and I was teasing him. I support Man United and my team are better than his!

'Your team is pants,' I told him.

'No, they're not!' complained Jason.

'We'll see,' I replied. 'We're playing you

soon so we'll find out who the best team are . . .' I said.

Dal and Chris groaned at the same time.

'What's up with you two?' I asked them.

'How many times do we have to tell you?' replied Dal. 'There is only one team – Liverpool!'

'Rubbish!' Jason said. 'Rubbish, rubbish, rubbish!'

I had taken my own ball to training and it was in a plastic bag in my hand. As I walked along, I was kicking the bag. We walked around a corner onto Ethel Road and in front of us were two lads, Gurinder and Ant, who used to play for our team. Both of them had left to join another team: Langton Blues – the team we were playing in our Cup-tie on Saturday! I wondered whether to say hello but decided that I didn't want to.

As we approached them, Ant smirked at us. 'Here come the girls!' he called out.

'Get lost!' replied Chris.

Dal told us to ignore them, but then Gurinder started having a go at us too.

'We're going to beat you on Saturday,' he said.

I looked at him and shook my head. 'You haven't got a chance,' I told him. 'The only reason you left was because the girls are better than you are.' Gurinder played in goal, so I went on: 'And Gem's a much stronger keeper.'

'No!' complained Gurinder.

'We're the best team in the league,' Ant added.

'Which league?' I asked. 'The Stupid League?'

'Come on, Abs!' Jason said to me. 'Let's just go . . .'

'Yeah,' said Ant, taunting us, 'you run away like little girls . . .'

I wanted to reply, but I didn't. Instead me

and my friends left Ant and Gurinder where they were. When they were out of earshot, I turned to my friends.

'We have to beat them on Saturday,' I said.

'We will,' said Chris determinedly.

When I got in I went straight up to my room. I sat down at my desk and thought about the Cup game against Langton Blues. It was the quarter-finals. We were only two games away from the final. And, no matter what, I was going to do my best to score against the Blues on Saturday and shut Gurinder and Ant up!

Chapter 2

Saturday

Our Junior Cup game was being played at our home ground and my older brother Mo – who had given me a lift – stayed to watch. We got there early and I went to speak to Wendy about our third coach, Steve. He'd been really poorly and I wanted to know how he was.

'He's a lot better,' Wendy told me.

'Will he be back soon?' I asked.

'No,' she said, looking quite sad. 'He's not going to be back for a while.'

I nodded and said that I wanted to go and see him.

'No problem,' she replied. 'We'll organize something next week.'

Behind Wendy, a man with a small camera was filming a woman talking about the game. The man and woman were called Hayley and John and they had been following the Reds for a few weeks. They were friends of Wendy's who were making a documentary about our team. I said hello to them when they had finished filming.

'Are you excited about playing in the Cup?' Hayley asked me.

I looked at John. He was filming me now. I was being interviewed!

'Yes,' I replied to Hayley with a smile.

'Do you think the Reds can win?'

'No problem,' I said, wanting to sound as confident as possible.

'And what sort of impact can the girls

have today?' Hayley continued. 'Langton are a good side. Can the girls help you to win?'

I nodded. 'I think that the girls are as good as any of the Langton players,' I replied. 'And some of them are better!'

Hayley beamed at me. 'Thanks, Abs!' she said.

''S OK,' I replied.

When I got back to my brother he was talking to Dal's dad. I looked for Dal but couldn't see him anywhere. Instead, I saw Chris and Jason and I joined them as they walked into the changing rooms.

'I can't wait for the game to start,' said Jason.

'Neither can I,' I replied.

'Do you think Ant and Gurinder will be playing?' asked Chris.

'I hope so,' I said. 'That way it'll be even better when we stuff them.'

But I wasn't too sure that we would beat

them. Langton Blues were one of the three top teams. We had only managed a 2–2 draw with them in the league – and I'd missed a penalty! It was going to be a tough game.

Out on the pitch, the whole squad got together for the team talk. Ian told us to focus on our own game.

'Forget what they're doing,' he told us. 'Play the game on the floor . . .'

'Pass and move!' urged Wendy.

'And try and keep tight in defence. I want to see everyone helping to defend and that includes the strikers!'

I looked at Chris who grinned.

'Now get out there and show them how much better you've become!' added Wendy.

We started the game with Leon, Dal, Steven – our captain – and Parvy in defence. Jason was in the midfield with Byron and Lily and Corky were the wingers. I was up front with Chris. We had five substitutes but none of them were goalkeepers. The only keeper in the squad since Gurinder had left was Gem so she went in goal.

Langton Blues were waiting for us as we took up our positions. I looked for Ant, but he wasn't on the pitch. Gurinder was playing though. He was standing on his goal line, rubbing his hands together.

'Let's put these girls out of the Cup!' I heard him yell.

As I started to shout something back, I saw Ian on the touchline put his finger up to his lips. He was telling me to shut up so I did. Two more of Langton's players, Beggsy and Luke, were standing near me. They had both played against us in our last game and I was desperate to show them that we were much better now.

'Oh, look!' said Luke. 'It's the Bratz team.' He had a piggy-looking nose and freckles and his hair looked like it had been stuck on with glue. In the last game Dal had told him that he looked like SpongeBob. Beggsy, who was their captain, started laughing at Luke's comment, but in our last game it had been Lily who had been the best player and she was a girl! I told them so.

'She won't be the best player this time,' replied Beggsy, looking really smarmy.

'We'll see,' I told him as the ref sounded the whistle.

We started the game slowly and there were no chances at all for the first ten minutes of the first half. Every time we got the ball we tried to pass it around but the Langton players were doing all they could to stop us. And whenever they got the ball, all they did was try and lump it forward to their strikers. But Dal and Steven won the ball every time and pretty soon I started to get frustrated.

I'd hardly touched the ball at all.

Suddenly the ball broke free in the centre of the pitch. I saw Byron run to get it and then pass it quickly to Lily. She had a defender close to her but he was too slow. She took the ball, skipped past him and headed down the left wing.

I turned and ran into a space in the box, taking two defenders with me. Lily looked up and curled in a cross. It sailed past me and the defenders and landed at Chris's feet. Chris controlled it well but didn't shoot. Instead he saw Gurinder running out of his goal to reach him. Chris twisted left and then right and then passed the ball into a space.

I turned my marker and stuck my foot out. The ball flicked up and looked like it was heading into the goal. I spun round to celebrate, but I was too early. The ball had hit the post!

Gurinder gathered it and threw it out. Then he called me some rude names. I ignored him and sprinted back to my position.

Five minutes later we made another attack. This time it was Corky and Parvy who created the chance. Corky passed to Parvy who passed it back to him. Then she ran down the right of the pitch and found a space. Corky saw her run and put the ball in front of her. She ran onto it, passed her defender and then squared to Lily. I went to Lily's left and Chris ran to her right. All she had to do was slip the ball to either one of us and we'd be through on goal.

But she didn't do that. Instead Lily held the ball and when a defender came to meet her, she put the ball through his legs and then smashed it towards the goal. I watched as Gurinder stretched to turn the ball away.

But he couldn't reach it. The ball rifled into the back of the net.

1–0!

The Langton players groaned and their captain, Beggsy, started shouting at Gurinder. Suddenly they were all arguing.

'I can't believe you let a girl score!' moaned Luke, the one with the freckles.

'Yeah!' I shouted. 'A girl!'

Gurinder told me to get lost and soon the game had restarted. Langton went on the attack straight away, with Beggsy and Luke trying their best to set up a goal. But we defended really well and Langton couldn't get near our goal.

Eventually – just before half time – the ball broke to Jason and he pushed it forward to Lily. She stepped inside her marker this time and passed the ball to me. I looked up and saw that Gurinder was off his goal line. I thought about shooting but decided that it would be better to pass to Chris who was shouting for the ball.

I turned, ready to kick it to him when I felt my legs go from underneath me. It was Luke!

Chapter 3

'FOUL!' I heard Lily shout as I cried out in pain.

But the referee didn't stop the game or give us a free kick. Instead he let Langton come away with the ball and very quickly Beggsy was running towards our goal. I sprang to my feet and tried to sprint back but my right leg really hurt. I managed to go about five metres before I fell to the ground. A shooting pain worked its way from my right foot up into my shin and knee. It was horrible!

As I sat down and rubbed my leg, I saw the ball being passed to Luke. He took two touches to control it and then ran into our box. Steven came towards him, but just as he was going to make his tackle, he slipped. Luke was free, one on one with Gem. He lashed at the ball and it skidded across the surface. Gem managed to get her left hand to it but it wasn't enough. Luke turned away to celebrate the equalizer.

It was 1–1.

'NO!!!!!!!' shouted Byron and Jason together.

'That's not fair,' complained Steven. 'Abs was fouled!' He was our captain and it was up to him to make the protest.

The referee waved him away, looked at his watch, then put his whistle to his lips and blew for half time. I stood up and hobbled from the pitch. Ian and Wendy were waiting for me.

'Are you OK?' asked Ian.

I nodded. 'It's just a bit sore,' I said. 'I'll be OK, honest.'

But I wasn't OK. I thought that the pain would go away only it didn't. But I really didn't want to be substituted. I wanted to play!

'Are you sure, Abs?' asked Wendy, as John walked over with his camera.

I nodded again. Suddenly another pain shot up my leg and I winced. I needed to sit down, but if I did Wendy would know that I was hurt. I thought about how much I wanted to play and score against the Blues. How I wanted the glory of putting my team into the next round of the Cup – the semi-finals.

But then I realized that if I played with an injury I wouldn't be able to play my best game. And that would put the team in trouble. I wanted to play on, but that would have been plain selfish. And I didn't want to let my team down.

'Actually, Wendy,' I said, 'I don't think I can play on . . .'

Ian told me to sit and went to get his bucket of water and sponge. When he got back he soaked the sponge and then held it against my injured leg. My brother, who had been talking to Jason's mum, saw what was happening and came running over.

'Are you OK, Abs?' he asked, looking concerned.

I nodded. 'I just got a bit hurt,' I replied. 'I can't play on.'

'Oh no!' Mo said, looking really disappointed for me. He knew how much I'd wanted to do well.

'Don't worry,' said Ian. 'It's just a bad knock. You'll be fit for the next game, no problem.'

Dal, Lily and Chris came to see what was up and I told them. They looked really upset.

Lily crouched down next to me.

'It was that horrible Luke,' she told me. 'That gerbil-faced, skinny cat poo!'

Dal and Chris grinned at what Lily had said.

'We have to score again,' she added seriously. 'I want to make sure that Luke goes home a loser.'

'Yeah,' agreed Chris, who had stopped grinning. 'We're going to win this game and stuff their cheating down their throats!'

Ian got the team together and told them the news. Penny was going on in my place. She was going to play out on the left wing and Lily was going up front with Chris. Ian also told Corky that he was coming off.

'We're going to swap you with your sister, son,' he told him.

For a moment Corky looked upset, but then he just nodded and said it was fine.

Olivia smiled and then she punched her brother on the arm.

'It's OK, isn't it?' she asked.

Corky nodded. 'Of course it is,' he told her. 'You're my sister . . . just make sure you play your best.'

'I will!' she replied.

I stood up with the help of my brother and walked over to the subs area. Some of the parents were there and so were the rest of the squad. Ian and Wendy led a team talk, and then, as I stood helpless on the side-lines, the team walked back onto the pitch.

'How are you going to win with even more girls?' taunted Beggsy. 'You were rubbish with three and now you've got five!'

'You're going out of the Cup,' added Luke.

I looked across at Ant. He was still not playing, but he didn't care. He smirked at me and then pulled a face.

'Come on,' I heard Lily shout to the other

girls on the pitch. 'Let's show these smelly boys what a soccer ninja really is!'

I smiled and started a chant in support of my friends. Pretty soon all the parents joined in too.

'COME ON, YOU REDS!' we all sang.

Chapter 4

The second half kicked off with Langton on the ball. It wasn't much fun watching from the sidelines, but I was doing my best to cheer my team on. The problem was that Langton kept hold of the ball for the first ten minutes and we hardly got a touch. And I was desperate to get back onto the pitch. As I couldn't, I just grew more and more frustrated.

Beggsy and Luke were playing really well and then, to make it worse, Ant came on.

He ran around teasing our players and I could see that my friends were getting more and more upset. At one point he ran past Lily and tried to pull her hair. Chris saw what he had tried to do and he complained to the referee. But the ref hadn't seen it and he told Chris to go away.

'REFEREE!' shouted Chris's dad, who was standing next to me.

'That was awful,' complained Jason's mum.

I nodded in agreement.

'Come on, Reds!' yelled Ian. 'Get the ball on the ground and play football! Pass and move . . .'

The Langton players kept kicking the ball up to their strikers. They weren't even trying to play properly. All they were doing was lumping it. It was boring to watch because they didn't really have any chances to score.

But then, about fifteen minutes into the

half, Dal managed to get the ball and run with it. He skipped a challenge from Beggsy and passed the ball sideways to Byron.

Byron pretended that he was going to play it to Lily but, just as his marker went to intercept the ball, he switched and played it to Penny instead.

'COME ON!' I shouted.

Penny gathered the ball and ran down the line, taking on the player in front of her. When he tried to tackle her, she avoided him and crossed into the box. Chris ran towards the ball. I think he wanted to head it, but it was too low and he had to readjust his feet. He volleyed it with his right foot. The ball flew towards the goal like a missile and hit the post. The sound it made was cool!

THWANG!

The Langton defence were all over the place. They were running around like ants. Not one of them knew where the ball was. It landed at Lily's feet. I thought she would shoot straight away, but she didn't. Instead she stayed really calm and side-footed it to Olivia, who had appeared from nowhere. Olivia hit the ball with all her might and it flew into the net. Gurinder had no chance!

It was 2–1!

'YESSSSSSSSS!!!!!!' I shouted with glee.

I gave my brother a high-five as Wendy and the rest of our supporters cheered.

'Calm down, Reds,' Ian called out. 'Concentrate . . .'

Now we were in the lead and there were only about ten minutes left to play. We had a chance to go through. A real chance! I was so excited. I wanted to jump up and down but my leg was still hurting. Two metres away from me, our substitutes were going crazy. Pete and Emma were doing a little dance and Ben was whooping in excitement.

The Langton players started arguing

amongst themselves. Beggsy was blaming Luke, Luke was blaming Ant, and their defence was having a go at Gurinder. They were so upset that they forgot to take up their positions properly for the restart. Immediately we were back on the attack.

Penny started it by running right at the heart of their defence. She ran past two players and then passed to Chris. He turned one way and then the other before squaring to Olivia. As I looked on in amazement, Olivia dribbled past three of their players. She was one on one with Gurinder. He ran off his line to try and stop her from scoring but that was his big mistake! Olivia waited until he had closed her down and slid the ball to Chris. Chris tapped the ball into an empty net.

3–1!

This time I couldn't stop myself from going crazy. I jumped up and down and nearly

forgot about my injury. All around me our supporters were doing the same thing. Even Hayley and David from the TV company were joining in. There was no way we were going to lose now! Langton Blues were out of the Cup and it was the Reds who were going to make the next round.

'RUSHIE . . . RUSHTON REDS!' sang my brother and Chris's dad together.

'COME ON, YOU REDS!' added Jason's mum.

Even Ian, who usually tries to calm us down if we score, was going mad. It was 3–1 and we were in the semi-finals of the Cup!

When the final whistle blew, the Blues trudged off the pitch angrily. They were all still blaming each other for their defeat. But I knew better than that. They had lost because they'd not played as a team. They had thought that our team would be weak because of the girls. But they had been wrong. We had outplayed them and been the better team! And now we were through and they were out!

Olivia walked over to me, smiling her head off. 'Told you!' she said.

'That was great play,' I replied. 'You're really good . . .'

She shook her head. 'I'm OK,' she said. 'But I know I can play better than that.'

As Dal, Lily, Chris and Jason joined us, I heard Gurinder's voice. He was shouting at someone. I turned around and saw that him and Ant were arguing.

'Serves them right for leaving the Reds!' said Dal.

'Absolutely, hubby dearest,' said Lily. She knew exactly how to wind Dal up!

'Please don't call me that!' complained Dal.

'Oh grow up,' replied Lily. 'Everyone

knows that you love me really . . .'

Dal went bright red as usual and I started to laugh my head off. It didn't matter that I hadn't played in the second half – I was still really happy. All that mattered was that the team had won. We were in the semi-finals and I was determined to be ready for the match. There was no way I was going to miss it.

Chapter 5

Tuesday

On Tuesday after school, Jason, Dal and Chris came with me to go and see our coach Steve at his house. He'd had a heart attack and been in hospital but was now getting better at home. Wendy had arranged for us to go, and she was meeting us there. My dad had finished work early and drove us there.

'I'm going to pop off and do some shopping,' he told us. 'I'll be back for you in an hour.'

'OK, Dad,' I replied.

We got out of the car and Dal walked forwards to knock on the door. Steve's house was quite big and it had a bright-red door with the number 18 in white letters on it. Wendy's car was already on the driveway. We were all a bit nervous about seeing Steve as we hadn't seen him since he'd been taken ill. It was Wendy who opened the door.

'Hey, lads!' she said cheerily. 'Come on in!'

She turned and led the way as we went in. Jason shut the door behind him. From the moment I walked in, I was amazed. Every wall had football stuff hanging from it. There were pictures and pennants and framed match-day programmes. I stopped to look at one. It was for a game between Liverpool and Manchester United. The date was 1977! That was ages ago.

'Wow!' I said. 'Hey, Jason – check these out!'

Jason was looking at another programme. This one was also from 1977. It had a cup on the front of it and when I looked more closely I saw that it was the Champions League trophy! But it wasn't called that then. It was called the European Cup. The programme was for the final and I couldn't pronounce the name of the team who had played Liverpool. The name read 'Borussia Moenchengladbach'. Work that one out!

'How cool are these,' replied Jason. 'Never mind that they're Liverpool programmes.'

'I bet these would cost a fortune on eBay!' I said.

'I bet you can't get them on eBay,' he replied.

I shook my head. 'You can get anything on eBay,' I told him. 'That's what my dad always says . . .'

'Can't buy me on eBay,' said Jason. 'Or you, Abs!'

'Oh don't be so silly!' I told him. 'That's not how I meant to say it . . .'

Jason grinned.

'Come on, lads!' said Wendy. 'Steve's looking forward to seeing you again.'

We stopped admiring the programmes and walked into the living room. Steve was sitting in a brown leather armchair. He had glasses on and a newspaper in his lap. His head was resting against the back of the chair. He was fast asleep!

'But he's—' I began.

'*SSSSHHH!!!*' replied Wendy, putting a finger up to her lips. 'He's just having a nap. He'll be awake again soon . . .'

'Is he sleeping because of his heart attack?' asked Dal.

Wendy nodded. 'He's been very, very poorly,' she told us, 'so he needs to get as much rest as he can.'

'Maybe we shouldn't have come,' I suggested.

Wendy shook her head. 'No, no, no . . .' she told us with a big smile. 'He really wanted you to, but the medicine he's taking makes him feel tired, so occasionally he has to take a nap.'

Dal grinned. 'Like Chris's cat,' he said. 'That cat is always asleep . . .'

I didn't even know that Chris had a cat. I turned, ready to ask him, but his face had dropped.

'I haven't got a cat,' he insisted.

'Yes, you have,' replied Dal, looking a little bit confused. 'It's always sitting on the windowsill in the living room. I've seen it!'

Chris looked even more upset. 'I haven't got one!' he repeated.

Wendy told him to calm down.

'Look,' she said to Dal, 'if Chris says he hasn't got a cat, then he hasn't.'

Dal shook his head. 'But he has got one!' he replied. 'Honest. I've seen it!'

'Chris?' asked Wendy.

Chris looked at us all and then he nodded. 'I *used* to have a cat,' he told us.

'See!' said Dal, getting excited.

'SSSHHH!' replied Wendy, pointing to Steve who was still asleep.

'Sorry,' said Dal.

Chris looked down at the floor. 'My dad let it go out the front one night and it got run over,' he revealed.

'Oh, I'm sorry,' said Wendy. 'That's horrible.'

Chris nodded. 'I wasn't at home when it happened,' he continued. 'I was staying at my Uncle Henry's with my mum and my sister, and my dad didn't tell us about it.'

'Oh,' said Jason. 'So how did you know?'

Chris sort of half smiled. 'He pretended that it had run away,' he told us. 'My mum was very upset because it was really her cat. So about three weeks later he went and bought her a new cat – a kitten.'

I looked at Dal and Jason. Both of them shrugged at me.

'So what about the cat on the windowsill?' asked Wendy.

'Well, my mum said she didn't want a new cat so the kitten had to go back. Then the next day my dad brought Barrington home,' Chris told her.

'Who's *Barrington*?' I asked, getting really confused.

'The first cat,' replied Chris.

'But didn't you say that Barrington was run over by a car?' said Jason.

Chris nodded.

'So how did your dad bring Barrington back then?' asked Dal.

46

Chris shrugged. 'He got him stuffed,' he admitted.

'*Stuffed?*' repeated Wendy, looking really shocked.

'Yes,' replied Chris. 'And my mum put it on the windowsill. After she'd stopped shouting at my dad which was for, like, *three* days.'

'That's gross!' said Jason. 'You've got a dead cat in your house! *Ehhh!*'

Chris shrugged. 'I don't *like* it being there,' he told us. 'But my mum was *really* close to Barrington and she wants to keep him and . . .'

'That's OK, Chris,' added Wendy. 'There's no need to explain anything to us. It was your mum's cat and she's entitled to have it stuffed . . .'

But even Wendy was smiling as she said it. It *was* funny. And *gross* too!

Chris shrugged again. 'My parents are a

bit strange,' he admitted.

'All parents are strange,' added Jason.

'And embarrassing,' I chipped in. 'My dad does really smelly farts all the time . . .'

'OK, lads, enough with the strange things that adults do – who wants a drink?'

We all put our hands up and followed Wendy into the kitchen. Steve's house was really big. And every wall had football souvenirs on it. They were mostly about Liverpool FC so Dal and Chris were much more excited than me, but I still looked at them. And that was how I found it out. Steve had played proper, real soccer! For a major team!

As Wendy made us orange squash, I called the lads over to the picture I was looking at. There were two rows of players in the photograph, the front row on a bench so that you could see the heads of each player. Underneath the photo it said: '*Reserve*

Division One Winners 1981–82 – Liverpool FC'.
And standing in the middle of the back row,
grinning out at us, was Steve!

'*OH MY GOD!*' said Chris.

'*NO WAY!*' said Jason. '*NO WAY, NO WAY,
NOOOO WAYYYY!*'

Wendy laughed at us. 'You really didn't
know, did you?' she said.

'You *knew?*' I asked.

She grinned. 'Yep!' she replied.

'But how come he never talks about it?'
I asked.

Wendy sighed. 'Steve never went past
that season as a pro,' she told us. 'He had a
really bad injury and had to give up. He left
and went into coaching instead . . .'

'That's just *sooo* crazy!' I replied. 'I can't
believe he played proper soccer!'

'Football,' corrected Jason. 'Soccer is an
American word.'

I looked at Wendy and grinned. '*Potayto,*

potarto!' I said before she could, but my American accent was rubbish.

It was a running joke – something Wendy had said when we'd first met her. I didn't mind if it was called football or soccer. It was still the same to me – brilliant! But as Wendy had told us over and over again, most of the rest of the world called it soccer. And 'soccer' was actually a British word anyway. I repeated all of this to Jason, but he didn't believe me or Wendy.

'So why is the FA called that then?' he asked. 'It's the *Football Association*.'

Someone coughed behind us. It was Steve. He was awake and he was smiling.

'It's called that because the words "football" and "soccer" are interchangeable,' he said.

I looked at my friends. I didn't have a clue what he meant. Wendy saw that we were all confused.

'It means that you can use either word,' she explained. 'Both mean the same thing.'

Steve walked slowly towards us. 'Hello, lads,' he said. 'So are you going to win the Cup for me then?'

Chapter 6

Saturday

Our next league game didn't excite me as much as the Cup. And that Saturday, we were going to find out who we would be playing in the semi-finals.

Our league match was against Rockwell Rangers, a team that we'd beaten earlier in the season. It had been our first win of the year. We were playing at home so I got there really early and changed into my kit. The coaches had given me a fitness all-clear after they'd seen me at training on Thursday, and I was well pleased I'd be playing again.

Once I got outside, I saw my dad standing chatting to Ian and Wendy. No one else had arrived yet. I ran over to the coaches.

'Who have we got in the draw then?' I asked, hoping that they'd tell me first because I was already there. But Ian shook his head.

'Not until the rest get here, Abs,' he told me. 'It's only fair.'

Fair? What did fair have to do with it? I was the first one there – surely I deserved to find out before the rest of the squad. But Ian refused to budge, so in the end I told him that I was going to practise my free kicks.

'Good!' he replied. 'Nice to see that you're so keen.'

I left the adults talking and walked across to the nearest goal. Wendy and Ian had fixed the nets already and I placed the ball I had with me about twenty yards from the goal. I wanted to practise curling the ball. I wasn't very good at it – and ever since I'd seen Lily do it, I had been desperate to match her.

I took four steps backwards and then ran to kick the ball. I connected with it well enough, but it didn't go anywhere near the goal. It went closer to the corner flag! Rubbish. I went and got the ball and ran back to my spot. I put the ball down again and this time I took five or six steps backwards. I started my run-up again, hoping to put the ball in the top left-hand corner of the goal. This time the ball was on target but it didn't go where I wanted it to.

I retrieved the ball and tried again. The third time I hit it, it flew! It swerved in mid-air and curled into the top corner. YES! I ran and got the ball, sprinted back to my position and did it again. The result was the same.

After five more goes, I stopped and began
to start warming up for the game. Lily and
Parvy joined me two minutes later and we
did little short sprints together. As we ran,
Lily asked me who we had in the next round
of the Cup.

'I don't know,' I told her. 'Ian wouldn't tell
me.'

'I bet we get someone really good,' she said.

'I don't care who we get,' Parvy told us. 'We'll beat them all.'

As we started on some more sprints, the rest of the team began to join us too. After we'd done a few turns, Wendy got us stretching our legs. Finally she asked us to gather together, just as the Rockwell Rangers team came out onto the pitch and began their warm-up.

'OK, Reds . . .' Wendy said, 'let's talk tactics.'

'But who've we got in the Cup?' asked Dal and Byron together.

Wendy shook her head. 'Never mind about that,' she told us. 'We need to concentrate on this game first. Now Ian and I have had a chat and we've decided to try something a little different today . . .'

I looked at Chris and Jason who were standing with me. What was Wendy talking about?

'At the last training session we tried playing with only three defenders,' she said. 'Three-five-two instead of four-four-two. What did you think of it?'

Nobody said anything for a moment and then Dal spoke up.

'It was OK,' he replied.

'Good,' said Wendy. 'Now we think that you should do really well today. Rangers aren't playing too well and we want you to really attack them.'

'YES!' shouted Lily.

'So we're going to play three at the back like at the training session. Steven, Dal and Parvy.'

There was a bit of murmuring but Wendy quietened us down.

'Leon will play out at right midfield with Corky on the left,' she said, looking at them both. 'Your job, lads, is to defend when required but to attack too. I want to see you getting in their faces. Pin them back and stop them from going forward. OK?'

Leon and Corky didn't seem sure, but both of them nodded.

'Right,' said Wendy. 'That leaves Jason and Byron in the centre midfield as usual.

And up front we'll start with Abs and Chris, with Lily playing just behind them as an extra central midfielder . . .'

'But Lily plays out on the wing,' said Emma.

''S OK,' Lily told her. 'I'll play wherever Wendy wants me to.'

Ian walked over and joined us. He'd been talking to the Rockwell Rangers coach and a few of the parents too.

'This is a very attacking game plan,' Wendy told us.

'Yes,' added Ian. 'And that means that we *must* concentrate. I want to see the ball on the ground – passing and movement. And when we lose the ball, I want to see everyone trying to get it back, OK?'

The entire squad nodded.

'And if you're a sub, keep yourself warm. Three of you will be getting a chance later on. Now get out there and show this lot what it means to be a Red!'

'COME ON, REDS!' shouted Byron. 'Let's get 'em!'

Chapter 7

I ran onto the pitch alongside Lily and Chris. Lily turned to me and grinned.

'Hey, Abs, first one to three goals!' she said. It was a challenge.

'Only if you let me take the first free kick, if we get one,' I replied.

'Done!' she told me, sticking out her hand for me to shake. I shook it.

The referee waited for everyone to get settled and then he blew his whistle to start the game. Rangers kicked off and tried to go on the attack, but Jason stopped their captain, Michael, with a brilliant tackle and gave the ball to Byron. He passed it to his right where Leon was waiting.

Leon is really quick and he sprang down the line like a cheetah! The Rangers players couldn't get near him. He ran right to the touchline and then turned to cross the ball. I thought he might put it in the air but he didn't. Instead he saw Lily and passed to her along the ground.

Lily had her back to her defender. She waited and waited, teasing him by moving the ball left and right. The second that the defender went in for the tackle, she flicked the ball between her legs, spun round and left him for dead. A second defender – a huge lad called Martin with really goofy teeth – ran at her. This time she didn't wait. As he approached her she looked up and saw that

I was free in the box, with my back to goal.

'ONE-TWO!' she shouted.

She flicked the ball to me. I watched her step around Martin and run into the space. I didn't try to control the ball. Instead, as another defender tried to tackle me, I passed the ball back to Lily. She was clean through on goal and she made no mistake. As the Rangers keeper advanced, she calmly passed the ball through his legs and into the goal.

1–0!

'YESSSSS!!!!!!' came a shout from our parents on the side of the pitch.

Lily went on a little run, holding her arms out like aeroplane wings. When I caught up with her she grinned and thanked me for the pass.

'No problem,' I told her.

'Next time I'll set one up for you,' she replied with a wink.

Lily wasn't joking either. Two minutes later we were on the attack again. This time it was Corky who beat his defender, out on the left. He pushed the ball inside for Byron to run onto. Byron controlled it and ran at the goal. As Martin tried to get to him, he squared the ball to Lily and once again she was clean through.

I sprinted to get into the space between her and Chris. She realized I was there and placed the ball right in my path. It was a brilliant ball and all I had to do was take on the goalie and blast it into the net . . .

Wham!

Once again, my legs were scythed out from beneath me. A big defender backed away, his hands up as he tried to look innocent but the ref was having none of it. A direct free kick, right on the edge of the box.

This was mine! As the defenders shuffled into place to form their wall, I placed the ball and took a few steps back, then I slammed it home, curling it right up into the top corner just like I'd practised. I whirled round to celebrate.

It was 2–0!

Five minutes later and we were 3–0 up! This time it was from a cross by Leon. Byron had been fouled out on the right. Leon sent the free kick sailing over into the Rangers penalty area. And there at the back post was Steven, who headed the ball home. We were absolutely stuffing Rangers and it was all because of our new system. It felt like we had double the number of players that they had. Every time I looked around there was one of my team-mates in space. It was great!

Half time came quickly and we didn't have much of a team talk at all. Ian just told us to keep playing and passing.

'Keep moving too,' added Wendy. 'Rangers can't cope with it.'

We started the second half with Emma coming on for Corky, Pete for Chris, and Penny replacing Byron, who had twisted his ankle. There were no goals for the first fifteen minutes, but then Penny set up Lily for her second and it was 4–0!

Five minutes after that, Pete took on four players and set up Lily for a hat trick. The game ended 5–0 and we had been *awesome!*

'Told you I'd get three,' Lily said to me as we left the pitch. 'That's soccer *ninja* magic, that is!'

I grinned at her. I hadn't really liked Lily when she first joined our team. I'd thought that girls were rubbish at football. But they were all great – and Lily was better than most of the boys that I knew. I had a feeling that we were heading for glory and Lily and the rest of the Barbies were going to help us get there.

'Great game!' said Wendy as we huddled after the match.

'Yeah,' said Ian. 'But keep focused because next week we've got our toughest game yet. We've drawn . . . Clarendon United in the Cup!'

No one said a word. Clarendon were a great team. And they'd already beaten us at the beginning of the season.

'That's going to be a really tough match,' Dal said to me.

I nodded. Dal was right. If the Rushton Reds were going to get to the Cup final, we were going to have to do it the hard way!

Chapter 8

Tuesday

'I don't believe you!' Parvy said to me at training.

'It's true,' I insisted.

I'd been telling her about Steve and how he had once been a real professional footballer.

'But he would be famous,' she replied.

I shook my head. 'He got a really bad injury and he had to stop playing,' I said.

'Wow!' added Penny, who was standing with us.

The weather had turned cold and horrible. It was raining and we were getting soaked. Wendy and Ian had us split into small groups. We were practising passing the ball to each other. They had us jogging up and down the pitch, at angles to each other, passing the ball. Each one of us had a number and we had to call out the number of the person we were about to pass to. It was hard work.

'You never stop thinking,' Ian told us. 'During a game you have to keep focused.'

I looked over at Chris and Dal and smirked. 'Ian?' I asked.

'Yes, Abs?'

I pointed at Dal and Chris. 'It's a bit hard to stay focused when I have to look at their ugly faces!' I joked.

The rest of the squad started laughing – except for Dal, Chris and Lily.

'Don't you dare call my husband ugly!'

replied Lily. 'He's not ugly – he's handsome and lovely . . .'

For a moment I thought that Lily was really upset but then she grinned and I realized that she was trying to wind me up. Dal went red. As usual. He told Lily not to call him her husband.

'Oh, don't be silly,' she told him. 'You know you love me!' She turned and pranced over to Jason. 'Or I might have to have another husband . . .' she teased. Now it was Jason's turn to go bright red. He really *did* fancy Lily!

Ian and Wendy grinned before Ian told us to be quiet and listen.

'The game against Clarendon will be tough,' he said. 'They are playing really well. But so are we. We know we can score goals and we know we can defend. We're going to have to do both in order to beat them.'

Wendy nodded. 'But we don't want to

overdo the training. Soccer is also about having fun. So this week we won't be training on Thursday . . .' she told us.

Half the team groaned and the other half cheered. I was one of the moaners. I loved training and I loved being with my team-mates. Training on Thursdays made Saturdays come more quickly too. And Saturdays were my favourite day of the week.

'OK, Reds,' said Ian. 'Let's get out of the rain and talk tactics inside.'

We all went off to get changed. Once we were done, we gathered together in the community centre, which sat behind our home pitch. No one knew what was going to happen as we had never had a team meeting to talk tactics before. We'd spoken about them but never seen Ian draw out things on a whiteboard. It looked really weird, with blue arrows for attackers and midfield and red arrows to show defenders.

Ian told us to talk amongst ourselves as he and Wendy went to get something from Ian's car.

'I don't understand that diagram,' said Parvy in a whisper.

'Nor do I,' admitted Penny.

I shrugged. It was time to wind the Barbies up with a joke!

'So much for *ninja* skills,' I said. 'It's really easy to see what Ian's doing.'

'If you're sooo clever, Abs,' replied Parvy, 'why don't you tell us what it means?'

'The red arrows are . . . erm . . . they're the girls and the blue ones are the boys!' I said, teasing them.

Parvy looked suspicious but Penny fell for it.

'Oh, really?' she said.

'Yeah,' I told her. 'It just means that the boys are better at attacking than the girls . . .' I added.

'Oh,' said Penny.

'Don't listen to him!' Parvy told her. 'Abs is just teasing you.'

Penny asked me if I was joking and I said no. But I couldn't stop grinning.

'You horrible, smelly, nasty, horrible . . . boy!' she complained.

'I was only joking,' I told her.

'Joking?' asked Parvy. 'Like when you run?'

I frowned. 'What's wrong with the way I run?' I asked.

Parvy shrugged. 'It's not me,' she said, seriously. 'Ian said it.'

Now I was starting to get worried. 'What did Ian say?' I asked.

'I'm not sure that I should tell you,' replied Parvy. 'It's quite serious and I think you should ask him . . .'

'But . . .' I began.

'He said that you need to get something to help you run better,' she added.

'What do I need to get?' I asked, getting really, really worried.

Parvy shrugged again. 'Nobody knows,' she said. 'It's a medical mystery.'

Now I was getting frustrated. 'What is?' I snapped. 'What's a mystery?'

Parvy and Penny began to grin.

'*Why you run like a chicken!*' Parvy yelled.

It took a few seconds but then I realized. I'd been trying to wind the Barbies up and they'd actually done it to me. I had really thought that there was something wrong with my running.

'Gotcha!' said Penny.

'Cabbages!' I replied. 'Smelly, mouldy, rat-bitten cabbages!'

Parvy and Penny gave me a funny look.

'Abs?' asked Parvy.

'Yes?'

'Why is it that every time you call people names, you use vegetables?'

I shrugged. 'Have you ever seen a cool vegetable?' I asked. 'They're all lumpy and smelly and they don't taste nice.'

Penny nodded. 'That's a good point,' she admitted. 'I don't like vegetables.'

Parvy shook her head. 'Yeah, but what about peas? Peas are cool!' she said.

'Peas?' I asked. 'Yuck! Peas are nasty . . .'

Parvy smiled. 'And carrots,' she added. 'Carrots are great. They look like little orange people with mad green hair . . .'

I looked at Penny.

'No, they don't look like people!' said Penny.

'They do if you draw faces on them with a felt tip,' replied Parvy.

'Hey?' I asked. 'When did you do that?'

Parvy shrugged. 'Last Christmas. I was bored and there were loads of carrots from my mum's allotment in the garage. I took one and drew a face on it. It was my friend –

I called it George . . .'

This time Penny looked at me. Her face said that Parvy was mental!

'George?' I asked. 'You called a carrot George?'

Parvy nodded, so I asked her why.

'Because I don't like Bob as a name,' she said, the weirdo.

Before things could get any stranger, Ian and Wendy returned. And behind them was Steve!

'Hello, Reds!' he said as everyone realized who it was.

'It's Steve!' I said excitedly.

Parvy shook her head. 'No – I called it George,' she said, still talking about the carrot.

But I just ignored her. I was more interested in finding out what Steve was doing at training. Was he back for good?

'OK, Reds . . . Steve has come in to see

you, so gather round,' said Ian.

We did as he asked and I found myself standing with Dal and Jason.

'I wonder what he's going to tell us?' asked Jason.

'I bet he's coming back!' I said.

'Hope so,' added Dal.

But when Steve started speaking we learned that he wasn't coming back to coach us. Not ever.

'I'm afraid that I just need the rest,' he told us. 'But that doesn't mean I won't be coming to watch you play . . .'

As he spoke his voice sort of changed and he coughed a lot. I felt really sad that he couldn't coach us any more. I wanted to do something to help him, but there was nothing that I could do.

'But can't you just do a little bit of training?' asked Jason.

Steve shook his head. 'I'm afraid not,

son,' he replied. 'I'm not allowed to.'

'But, Steve—!' began Dal.

'It's OK,' Steve told us. 'Just go out there and win the Cup for me. That'll make me happy . . .'

Me and my best friends all looked at each other. Lily and her friends looked around too. Every single Red in the room wore a serious face. A *determined* face. I put up my hand to speak.

'Yes, Abs?' asked Steve

'We are going to win the Cup,' I told him.

'Do you mean you're going to try your best?' he replied.

'No,' said Parvy from behind me. 'I think what Abs means is that we are going to win.'

Steve kind of gulped and looked at Ian and Wendy.

'Tell the television people to bring lots of film,' added Byron. 'There are going to be loads of goals!'

Chapter 9

Saturday

Saturday came around so quickly. One minute I was on my way home after Tuesday's training, the next I was standing in the wind and the rain, waiting for the semi-final to start.

Ian had picked a strong team. We had Gem in goal, with a back four of Leon, Dal, Steven and Parvy. In midfield, Byron and Jason were central, with Corky on the right and Lily playing left wing. I was up front with Chris. Four-four-two. We were all really confident that we'd do well. But the last time we'd played them, Clarendon United had beaten us. And they had beaten us well. The Cup semi-final was our chance to show how much better we'd got. And to show our coach Steve how much we'd learned from his coaching. Wendy had brought Steve to the match with her. He wasn't going to miss this match!

Wendy then gathered us in a huddle before kickoff.

'Try and keep it tight at the back,' she'd said. 'Don't take too many risks and make sure you defend as a team.'

Now, as we faced the Clarendon players, all I could think about was Steve. I still couldn't believe that he was never going to coach us again. We'd only had one season as Rushton Reds and we'd lost one of our coaches. We'd also lost lots of players to other teams. And then there was all the teasing that we'd taken. All because we had girls in our squad. I wanted to win the Cup for all of those reasons. I wanted to show everybody that we deserved the glory. All of the Reds – the boys, the girls and the coaches too.

The referee blew his whistle and the game started. There were loads of fans for both sides cheering the players on. And Wendy's television friends were also there with their cameras – they'd followed us through the season and they were rooting for us too now.

Clarendon got on the ball quickly and began to pass it around. For about five minutes we were chasing shadows. Then there was a break in our midfield and one of their players, a lad called Sanjay, came away with the ball.

He ran at Dal and Steven at pace. Steven stepped out to meet him, but Sanjay's momentum was too strong and he nudged past Steven like he wasn't there. Dal tried to get to him but Sanjay played the ball square to one of their strikers, Marcus. Marcus turned and fired a shot at our goal. But Gem saw it coming and she blocked it. The ball bounced away and into Sanjay's path again. This time he tried to run around Gem. But she blocked him and managed to get to the ball.

She got up quickly and ran to the edge of her area. She threw the ball to Jason, who turned and passed it quickly to Lily, out on the left. Lily took two touches and then cut inside her defender, leaving him on his backside. She skipped another challenge and ran for the box.

I saw my chance. I told Chris to go for the near post, which he did. The defenders both went with him. That left me free at the back post and Lily passed me the ball. I controlled it and then lifted it over their advancing keeper.

It was 1–0!

I didn't celebrate though. I just ran back to my position and focused, like Ian had told us to do. The rest of the Reds did the same.

The game restarted with a free kick to Clarendon. Parvy had fouled their winger and she was apologising to him. The winger told her to get lost and Byron heard. He ran over and started shouting at the lad. But then Steven grabbed him and moved him away. The ref told Byron off and then

Sanjay took the free kick.

We thought he'd play it into the box because Clarendon's strikers were taller than our defenders. But he played it short instead, to a lad called Will. Will was short with spiky black hair and he had his socks rolled down. I remembered him from the first game. He had quick feet and could dribble really fast.

I sprinted back, hoping to help my defence out. But Will was far too quick. He skipped past Parvy's challenge and made it to the by-line. There he unleashed a wicked cross which landed right at the feet of Marcus, the striker. Marcus slammed the ball home.

It was 1–1!

The Clarendon players ran to the goal-scorer and jumped on him. They were cheering and whooping like they'd already won the game. But it was only 1–1 and we had a lot more left in us.

I turned to Chris. 'Let's try and get at their centre backs,' I told him.

'Yeah,' he agreed. 'They're a bit slow, so I reckon we can beat them.'

I grinned. 'Let's do it!' I replied.

But for the next ten minutes we couldn't get near the ball. Every time our defence managed to clear an attack, Clarendon started another one. I tried my hardest to get back and help out, but Ian shouted at me to hold my position.

'Keep the shape, Abs!' he was shouting. 'Give them an outlet . . . !'

I could see what he meant too. If I had gone back to defend, then we'd only have Chris up front against four defenders. That would put us under even more pressure. So I stuck with my position but still got frustrated. And it only got worse because Clarendon scored again.

It started with a mistake from Lily. She lost the ball in midfield and it was seized by Sanjay. This time he attacked Leon and beat him too. As Dal put in a challenge, Sanjay fed the ball to Marcus. He swivelled and blasted the ball into the net to make it 2–1 to them!

'NO!!!!!!!' groaned half of the Reds.

The Clarendon players ran to their coach to celebrate.

'WE'RE GONNA WIN THE CUP, WE'RE GONNA WIN THE CUP!!!!' they sang.

* * *

Five minutes later and it was 3–1. This time
they played a great move and beat us fair
and square. We couldn't get near to them
and Will, the little one with the rolled-down
socks, scored with a great shot. In the past
I would have moaned about the goal and
tried to blame someone. But not this time.
I could see the faces of my team-mates.
Everyone looked gutted. We had honestly
believed that we had a great chance of
winning the game. But we were getting
beaten and it didn't feel good.

We all trudged off slowly at half time. No
one was excited any more, no one was
chatting. I went over to the touchline and sat
down. What were we going to do? Wendy
passed around orange slices as Ian talked
to us.

'That was difficult,' he told us. 'They're
playing well. But we have to believe.'

Byron asked him what we had to do next.

Ian smiled. 'Firstly,' he told us, 'we need to get some goals so we're switching to three-five-two like we did in the last game. You midfielders must back up the defence when necessary – they're a strong team – but should also be ready to move forward and put the pressure on. Emma is coming on for Corky and we'll make more substitutions later. Secondly, we're all going to believe . . .'

'Huh?' said a load of us together.

Ian nodded. 'Yes,' he told us. 'We're going to believe – because if you believe in yourselves, then *anything* is possible. *Anything*.'

Wendy agreed with him. 'Who remembers Liverpool versus AC Milan in the Champions League Final a few years ago?' she asked.

Dal, Chris and Emma all put up their hands.

'Did they let their heads drop?' asked Wendy.

'NO!' shouted Dal and Chris together.

'Did they mope about like losers?' she said.

'NO!' said three quarters of the team.

'Did they go and do what everyone thought was impossible?' she added.

'YES!!!!!!' shouted everyone.

Wendy grinned. 'So go out there and do it, y'all!' she ordered.

Chapter 10

From the kickoff Clarendon didn't know what to do. Our system had changed and we were on the attack. We were winning all the tackles and getting to all of the loose balls first. Byron and Jason worked like demons in the middle, breaking up Clarendon's play and passing the ball well. It was great. But with ten minutes left to play we still hadn't scored.

Then Ian did something really brave. He took off Parvy and Leon and replaced them with Ben and Penny. Two defenders off and two attackers on. Byron moved into the three-man defence and Ben joined me and Chris up front.

Ben hadn't played much and, although he was really good in training, we hadn't seen much of him on the pitch. All of that changed though, seconds after he came on. Jason won the ball again and looked up. I ran to his left and Chris went right. Jason gave the ball to Ben instead. Without looking up, Ben ran at the Clarendon defence. He swerved this way and that way, left and right, until he'd made all the Clarendon defenders dizzy. And then, just when any other player would have shot at goal, he passed left to Lily and gave her an easy tap-in.

3–2!

Once again we didn't celebrate. We'd pulled one back, but we still needed at least one more. Lily grabbed the ball and ran back to the centre circle. She placed the ball for the Clarendon players and took up her position. Sanjay and Will laughed at her.

'What's the matter?' Sanjay asked her. 'Lost your lipstick?'

Lily smiled at him. 'Make way for the *ninja*,' she said.

'Huh?' replied Sanjay.

But Lily didn't say another word. Instead, as soon as Will kicked off, she ran in and nicked the ball, before Sanjay could get to it. She was so quick that Sanjay didn't even move. And when he did react, she was gone! She tore down the wing like a hare, and no one could stop her. I'd never seen her move so fast. I sprinted for the box, knowing that I'd have a good chance of scoring if she could get the ball to me. I moved into a space and tried to get her attention. Instead of passing to me, she gave it to

Chris, who turned his defender inside out. He was clean through on goal.

'SHOOT!!!!!!!' yelled Jason from behind me.

But Chris didn't shoot. He waited and then pretended to pass the ball to his left. Only he didn't actually pass the ball. Instead he rolled it left, under his foot, and then sent it the other way, sliding it across to Ben on his right!

The Clarendon defence didn't know what had hit them. They had all moved to the left and Ben calmly scored the equalizer.

3–3!

That was it. Our supporters went crazy. They were jumping up and down on the sidelines. Even Wendy joined in. And Ian just stood where he was, with his arms folded. But unlike in the past, he was actually smiling. A big, wide, mega-grin. Next to him, Steve's grin was even bigger!

'ONLY ONE TEAM GOING TO WIN THIS GAME!' shouted Wendy.

And she was right. Clarendon put us under pressure from the restart but the shot from Marcus, when it came, was weak. Gem gathered it up and threw it to Penny, who ran with it. She avoided two tackles and then passed inside to Emma. Emma turned her marker and found herself in space. She could have passed it to Jason. It would have been the easiest pass to make.

But Emma had other things on her mind. She played the ball, with the outside of her left foot, to Lily who was right on the touch-line. Lily gathered the pass and then teased her marker. The lad kept thinking he could win the ball but every time Lily showed it to him, she took it away just as quickly. She was making him look like a donkey! Finally, as the lad grew exasperated, she flicked the ball over his head and then ran around him.

He was so gutted that he didn't even try to stop her after that.

Like a flash she was in the box, and once again she ignored Jason and Chris and passed it across to Penny.

Penny took on her defender and squared it for Emma. Emma waited for a defender to make his move and she passed inside to Lily. Then Emma ran into the space and took the ball back.

I saw my chance. I ran for the back post. A big defender stood next to me. He was nudging me, trying to get me off-balance. But I held my ground. Emma pretended to shoot but then flicked the ball with her instep to Lily. My marker saw the move and tried in desperation to stop Lily getting a free shot on goal. But that was his mistake!

Lily flicked the ball up into the air. I could see it coming in my direction. I watched it, concentrating on it, until it was right where I wanted.

I lashed the shot home!

4–3!!!!!!

The game was surely over. We had to win now. There were, like, ten seconds left to play. I raced for my coaches with the rest of the team right behind me. When I got to Ian I jumped into him. One by one, the other Reds did the same. We were ecstatic!!!!!! And Steve was punching the air in triumph!

Seconds later the referee blew for full time. Lily and Dal grabbed me and hugged me.

'Welcome to the Soccer *Ninja* Club!' Lily said to me.

'YESSSSSSSSSSSSSSS!!!!!!!' I screamed.

We'd done it! The most teased team in the league. A team full of girls. A team that kept losing its players. A team that had lost its

most experienced coach. And yet we were now in the Cup Final. The Rushton Reds had proved their critics wrong.

We were on our way to glory!!!!!!!

'COME ON, YOU REDS!!!!' we all sang. 'COME ON, YOU REDS!!!!!!'

ABOUT THE AUTHOR

Bali Rai thinks he is a very lucky man. He gets to write all day if he wants to, or go into schools to speak to his readers about what they think of his books. He loves films, music, reading, seeing friends and watching his beloved Liverpool FC.

Bali played for his school team as a defender and loved it. He has been a lifelong football fan since he began watching Match of the Day at the age of four with his dad. He enjoys talking and arguing about Liverpool FC, and would like to be Rafa Benitez's or Steven Gerrard's personal servant, but if this does not happen he is happy to carry on writing for his thousands of fans.

Bali was very honoured that his short novel *Dream On* (about a young footballer) was chosen for the first Booked-Up list and was made available to every Year 7 school child.

Bali's books are now in ten languages and he gets to travel all over the world to meet his readers. He hopes that he can encourage anyone to have a go at writing and to find a love of reading. He has won lots of book awards and really enjoys winning the ones that are voted for by the real readers – you!

Bali lives in his home city of Leicester .
He has a lovely wife and a
football-crazy daughter.

Bali Rai

STARTING ELEVEN

'Come on!' I shouted to my team-mates.
'Let's start playing!'

The local youth club are putting an under-elevens squad
together – and Dal, Chris, Abs and Jason are determined
to be picked. They know they're the best players in their
school – but what if that isn't good enough and they
don't make the team? Dal knows he'd be gutted if his
mates made it and he didn't . . .

The first in a fantastic new football series from an author
with real street cred!

978 1 862 30654 7

Bali Rai

MISSING!

'COME ON, YOU REDS! COME ON, YOU REDS!'

Jason, Dal, Abs and Chris joined Rushton Reds – a new youth club squad – at the beginning of the season, but the team have lost their first two matches! They're all brilliant players, but they're missing chances all over the place. Jason has even missed a penalty . . .

Gripping football action from award-winning author Bali Rai.

978 1 862 30655 4

Bali Rai

STARS!

'Who's getting too big for his boots?'

Ruston Reds are going to be famous! A TV documentary
is being made about the team and Chris, Dal, Abs and
Jason can't wait to show off their skills in front of the
cameras. But is it more important to look like a star – or
to play well as part of the team?

Will fame go their heads . . . ?

Thrilling football action from award-winning
author Bali Rai.

978 1 862 30657 8